Basketball Stars!

Adapted by
Claire Smith

Learn Phonics with Peppa Pig

Phonics teaches children to read by learning the sounds of a language. They start by learning the sound for each letter or combination of letters, which helps them to break down words into sounds (**th-i-nk**). They can then blend these sounds together to read whole words ("think"). This is called sounding out and blending.

As children learn more sounds, they will meet them in lots of different combinations. With practice, they will learn to sound out and blend the sounds together to read new words.

Listen carefully as your child reads the **Learn with Peppa** stories with you. Encourage them to sound out and blend each word. If they find a word difficult, help them to sound it out. Most importantly, have fun!

Drag your finger along each line. Say each sound as you do so, and then blend the sounds together to read the whole word. At this level, your child will start reading words where two, three or four letters make one sound. Here, three letters together make one long vowel sound.

sh are
_ _ _

Find more phonics resources, guidance and audio online:

www.learnwithpeppa.com

Basketball Stars!

Read the sounds

Practise sounding out and blending to read these words.

a c ti o n

a t m o s ph ere

ch ee r s

e x p l o si o n

kn ee s

n eigh b our

n u mb

o b ey

o r a n ge

p o s i ti o n

r oar s

s c ore

Practise the words

These words cannot be sounded out in this way. Read them with your child.

do	friends	many	Mr	of
one	our	parents	says	shoes
the	through	to	today	were

Meet the friends

This name is not as easy to sound out and blend! Read it with your child.

Madame Gazelle

Madame Gazelle has a special surprise for the children today. They have all changed into their gym kits and sports shoes and gathered on the basketball court.

Madame Gazelle gives them instructions on how to warm up before they start to exercise. "You need to do this to stop your limbs from getting sore."

As Peppa Pig and her friends stretch, Daddy Pig appears at the edge of the court.

"Why is Peppa's daddy here in his gym kit?" asks Danny Dog.

"I taught Daddy Pig how to play basketball when he was a little piggy!" explains Madame Gazelle. "Now he's going to teach you!"

Daddy Pig spins an orange basketball on his finger. He makes a great impression on Peppa's friends!

"I was top scorer on my college basketball team, you know. We won many competitions," boasts Daddy Pig.

Under Daddy Pig's supervision, the training session begins.

"In basketball," says Daddy Pig, "we have to bounce the ball a lot. You try."

The children obey. Soon, they are busy bouncing up and down the court.

"More!" calls Daddy Pig.

"All this bouncing is making my hand go numb," grumbles Danny, with an unhappy expression.

"The next stage of training is passing to your neighbour," says Daddy Pig.

George and Richard Rabbit ignore Daddy Pig and kick the ball instead!

Daddy Pig motions towards the basketball hoop.

"To score," he explains, "you throw the ball straight through this large hoop."

Daddy Pig gets in position, bends his knees, and throws!
The ball soars through the air. Daddy Pig scores!

They all take turns. Rebecca Rabbit scores on her eighteenth try!

"You persevered, Rebecca," says Daddy Pig. "Well done!"

Next, George has a go. The ball soars backwards and just misses Daddy Pig's forehead!

Daddy Pig is coming to the conclusion that George is not ready for basketball.

Daddy Pig urges the children to pay attention.

"Your parents will be here soon for a match," he explains.

Daddy Pig has a team discussion. They come up with a plan of action.

"We won't let you down, Coach Daddy Pig," says Danny.

When the parents arrive, the atmosphere is electric.
The tension builds until Daddy Pig blows his whistle.

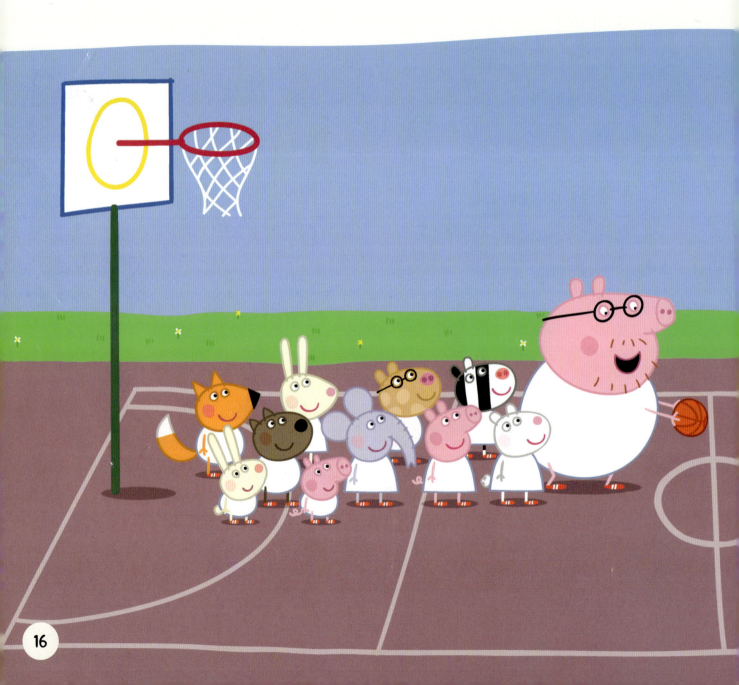

The match has begun! Mr Elephant gets the ball and dodges past Pedro Pony and Danny.

Zoe surges towards Mr Elephant. He drops the ball!

In one smooth motion, Zoe Zebra picks it up
and passes to Peppa.

Peppa passes the ball to George – can he rise to the occasion?

He shoots. He scores!

Daddy Pig blows his whistle again. That's the sign that the competition is over.

There is a huge explosion of cheers and roars!

Well done, George!

"You were our inspiration, Daddy!" says Peppa.

Daddy Pig feels emotional to hear Peppa say this.

"It was my pleasure!" he replies.

Have fun with Peppa Pig

A Answer these questions about the story.

1 Who taught Daddy Pig how to play basketball?

2 How did Daddy Pig impress Peppa's friends?

3 Why didn't Danny enjoy bouncing the ball?

4 Was Daddy Pig right when he thought George wasn't ready to play basketball?

5 Read page 11 again. Which words have the **ai** sound in them?

6 Which sentence on page 15 tells you that the team have decided what to do during the match?

B

Which team sport do you like playing the most? Is it fun to be part of a team? What do you like best about it?

Tell me a story

You can be a storyteller! Make up a new story that starts with what you can see in this picture.

LADYBIRD BOOKS

UK | USA | Canada | Ireland | Australia | India | New Zealand | South Africa
Ladybird Books is part of the Penguin Random House group of companies
whose addresses can be found at global.penguinrandomhouse.com.
www.penguin.co.uk   www.puffin.co.uk   www.ladybird.co.uk

Adapted from:
Peppa Pig: Peppa Plays Basketball first published by Ladybird Books Ltd 2016
Learn with Peppa Pig edition published by Ladybird Books Ltd 2023
001
© 2023 ABD Ltd/Ent. One UK Ltd/Hasbro

Adapted by Claire Smith
Phonics consultant: Charlotte Raby

PEPPA PIG and all related trademarks and characters TM & © 2003 Astley Baker Davies Ltd and/or Entertainment One UK Ltd.
Peppa Pig created by Mark Baker and Neville Astley. HASBRO and all related logos and trademarks TM & © 2023 Hasbro.
All rights reserved. Used with Permission.

Licensed by

Printed in China

The authorized representative in the EEA is Penguin Random House Ireland,
Morrison Chambers, 32 Nassau Street, Dublin D02 YH68

A CIP catalogue record for this book is available from the British Library

ISBN: 978-0-241-57721-9

All correspondence to:
Ladybird Books, Penguin Random House Children's
One Embassy Gardens, 8 Viaduct Gardens, London SW11 7BW

MIX
Paper from
responsible sources
FSC® C018179

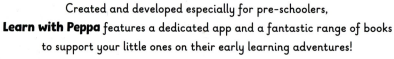

Created and developed especially for pre-schoolers,
Learn with Peppa features a dedicated app and a fantastic range of books
to support your little ones on their early learning adventures!

www.learnwithpeppa.com